There Is A Bike In My Bed

By JJ Brobbey

Illustrated by usillustrations.com

2023

This book is dedicated to my entire family. I love you all. Special shout out to my husband Kwadwo, your support is appreciated more than you know. My sons Deacon and Kaiden, thank you for your daily inspiration. My niece Tenae Michelle, thanks for the title. To the one who loved me "more than the whole outside", my father, thank you for the best surprise of my childhood, a bike in my bed.

Love,
Meatball
AKA
JJ Brobbey

Grace loved to eat. Spaghetti and meatballs was her favorite meal. It had been her favorite meal for as long as she could remember. One night, after eating her favorite dinner, her favorite uncle Jordan called her "Meatball." Grace loved the nickname so much, everyone has called her Meatball ever since.

Meatball had been wanting a bike for a long time. Every day during the summer she practiced riding her best friend Bern's bike. Meatball and Bern had lived on the same street since they were born. They were like two peas in a pod. They would take turns riding Bern's bike from the blue house next door, to Mrs. Ashley's house, to the funny brown house on the corner next to the candy store. They did not dare turn the corner. They had been warned by their parents not to leave the street.

Candy Shop

One afternoon when they had finished riding, it was time for lunch. Meatball's mom was in the kitchen washing dishes. As Meatball washed her hands to prepare to eat she asked, "Mom, when will I get my own bike? I'm tired of riding Bern's."

Her mom chuckled. "What do you know about being tired young lady?" she asked. Then, with a dishcloth in one hand, and the other hand on her hip, Meatball's mom recited all the things she had done while Meatball was outside riding Bern's bike from the blue house next door, to Mrs. Ashley's house, to the funny brown house on the corner next to the candy store.

Meatball knew where this would lead. She covered her eyes with her hands as if she could hide. She knew her mom was going to ask her about making her bed. That day, Meatball had hopped out of bed, brushed her teeth, dressed, and eaten her favorite fruity cereal as fast as she could so she could go outside to play with Bern. And just like every other day, her mother had yelled, "Did you make your bed?" just as she got to the door.

Meatball stomped back towards her bedroom. "You keep stomping your feet young lady and you'll be in here with me all day!" her mom yelled from the kitchen. Meatball apologized quickly and rushed to her room. The quicker she made the bed, the quicker she could go riding.

Bern was already outside. Meatball could hear her through the bedroom window. They had invented their own special call so they could speak to each other from their bedroom windows at night. The call was a cross between a bird and a giraffe. Neither of them had ever heard a giraffe before, but that was their favorite animal. Bern called for Meatball. She had a feeling Meatball was in her room making her bed.

Meatball made the bed as fast as she could. She did not understand why making the bed was such a big deal. She planned to ask her mother that question, but not today. Today all she wanted to do was hurry outside. She was super excited because it was her turn to ride Bern's bike first, from the blue house next door, to Mrs. Ashley's house, to the funny brown house on the corner next to the candy store.

That evening, after she brushed her teeth and changed into her favorite purple pajamas with red stars on them, Meatball prayed for God to send her a bike. Before dozing off, she pictured herself riding her bike between the blue house next door, to Mrs. Ashley's house, to the funny brown house on the corner next to the candy store. Meatball dreamed about the same thing. When she woke up the next day, she felt as if her dream was real. She remembered the bike clearly. It was red, with red, black, and white tassels on the handlebars. The tires were white with black trim. It was the best bike anyone could ever imagine.

When she realized it was only a dream, Meatball was very disappointed. She crawled out of bed, less enthusiastic than usual. She was on her way to the bathroom to wash her face and brush her teeth when she saw her parents sitting at the kitchen table having coffee.

"Good morning!" her parents said.

"Good morning," Meatball mumbled.

"What's wrong, Baby Girl?" Her dad always called her Baby Girl even though she was seven, and practically a grown-up. Meatball didn't mind. Her father was her favorite person on the whole planet. He was fun. The two of them were always laughing together. He would often tickle her until she laughed so hard she couldn't breathe. Her dad could call her Baby Girl as much as he wanted.

5

Meatball sighed. "Nothing's wrong, Daddy.
"I know when something is wrong with my Baby Girl," he said, looking at her with his head tilted to one side. "You can tell me."
Meatball sat on his lap and told him about her dream and how she woke up disappointed because it wasn't real.
"Daddy, will you please get me a bike?" she pleaded.

"Have you been a good girl, helping your mom around the house?" he asked. Meatball put her head down. She knew the subject of making her bed would come up. She decided it was the perfect time. She asked her mother why it was so important to make the bed at all.

"I'm just going to mess it up again when I get back into it at bedtime," she declared. Her father smirked, but her mother was not at all pleased that Meatball had questioned her.

"You'd be amazed how much better it feels to get into a bed that's been made when it's bedtime," her mom said. Then she added, "And because I said so, young lady." Meatball didn't like that answer, but she was smart enough to drop the subject so she could finish getting ready.

17

Today was a day she looked forward to every summer. It was the day of the annual church picnic. There was so much to love about the picnic, from the singing on the bus on the way there, to playing any game you could imagine once you got there, to endless tables of food including the sweetest strawberries she had ever tasted. Meatball loved strawberries, probably because they were red, and red was her favorite color.

Meatball pulled on her denim shorts and put on her favorite red sneakers with the sparkly laces. Next, she put on the bright yellow church t-shirt her parents had bought. Everyone at the picnic would be wearing one. It made it easier to see anyone from the church from anywhere in the park. Meatball thought the t-shirt went perfectly with her sneakers.

She walked toward the door to her bedroom and was about to turn off the light when she realized she had forgotten her jump rope. Meatball would not dare go to the picnic without it. She got it out of the toy box, then remembered she had not made her bed. She rolled her eyes and walked over to it.

"It's my bed," she grumbled. "Why can't I just leave it the way I want?" Meatball finished making her bed in less than five minutes. She was amazed that it did not take very long at all. She fluffed the pillows for an added touch. She knew her mom would like that. Bern's special call floated in from the bedroom window. Meatball bolted for the door.

Her mom was on the porch waiting for the church van. Meatball kissed her on the cheek. To her surprise, her mom did not mention making the bed. Meatball paused for a second. She started to ask, "Aren't you going to ask me about making the bed?" but decided not to. She figured her mom would see her bed and be pleasantly surprised.

Meatball heard the church van blowing its horn as it approached her house. She jumped down the porch steps two at a time. Bern was already running towards the van. She was running so fast it was as if she had on roller skates!

As always, the picnic was so much fun. They ran. They played. Meatball and Bern slid onto the bases during so many games of kickball that they both got grass stains on their shorts. Oh, and the strawberries! Meatball ate so many she could barely sing with the others on the ride home.

When the van pulled up in front of the house, her parents were waiting on the porch. Meatball waved goodbye to Bern. As they walked into the house, Meatball's parents asked her about the picnic. She shared every detail. She told them about all the fun she'd had, and all the strawberries she'd eaten. Mom gave Meatball The Mom Look. She was always talking to her about etiquette and sharing. Meatball grinned and explained that she didn't eat all the strawberries (even though she had tried to)!

After a moment, Meatball's father said, "You were in such a rush that you didn't make your bed this morning." His voice was stern.

"But I did make my bed," said Meatball, confused.

Her dad pointed toward her room. "Go make your bed. Now!"

25

Meatball turned slowly. She was shocked that her dad had yelled at her. She was even more shocked that he had not called her Baby Girl. She stomped toward her room.

Meatball opened her bedroom door. She looked at her bed. The blanket was all messed up, and there was something under it. She ran to the bed, threw back the blanket, and there it was.

A brand-new bike!

Meatball was so happy and excited that she screamed with joy. She ran back to her parents to give them both the biggest hugs. Then she grabbed her mom's right hand, and her dad's left hand, and lead them back into her room. She needed help to get the bike out of her bed!

The bike was exactly like her dream. It was red. It had black, red, and white tassels on the handlebars. It had white tires with black trim. It was her dream come true!

At bedtime, Meatball realized the bed had not been made after the bike had been removed. And she realized that her bed was more comfortable to get into after it had been made. She thought of her mom and smiled. That night, as she said her bedtime prayers, she thanked God for listening and for giving her the best bike a girl could have. She also thanked Him for giving her the best parents, too.

Meatball could not wait to show Bern her new bike in the morning. She could not wait for the two of them to ride their bikes together from the blue house next door, to Mrs. Ashley's house, to the funny brown house next to the old candy store.

The End